WRITTEN BY
RENNIE BROWN
ILLUSTRATED BY
STEVIE HALE-JONES

CHICKS
ROCK!

First published by Parragon in 2007

Parragon
Queen Street House
4 Queen Street
Bath BA1 1HE, UK

Copyright © Parragon Books Ltd 2007

ISBN 978-1-4054-9518-9
Printed in China

Fashion Model

PaRragon

Bath · New York · Singapore · Hong Kong · Cologne · Delhi · Melbourne

Installing and running your CD-ROM

Check out the cool fashion ideas in this book,
then follow the instructions below and get ready to start
designing some super-cool styles on your CD-ROM.

USING A PC:

1. Put the CD into the CD drive.
2. Double click on "my computer."
3. Double click on the CD drive icon, "Fashion Model."
4. Double click on the "start pc" icon.
You will see a loading icon and your CD will start.

USING APPLE MACINTOSH®:

1. Put the CD into the CD drive.
2. Double click on the CD drive icon, "Fashion Model."
3. Double click on the "start osx" icon if running on an OSX system or "start classic" if running on OS 9.2. You will see a loading icon and your CD will start.

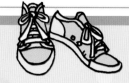

This CD-ROM will work on most PCs or Apple Macintosh® computers. Please consult the system requirements below for detailed specifications.

PC: WINDOWS 98 / 2000 / ME / XP

* Win98, Pentium II processor / Win2000, WinXP, WinME Pentium III processor
* CD-ROM drive
* Sound card
* Monitor displaying at least 800 x 600 pixels in 256 colors or higher
* 128MB of Ram (256 MB recommended.)

APPLE MACINTOSH®: CLASSIC / OsX

* Power Macintosh G3 500 MHz or higher Running a minimum OS 9.2 / recommended Mac OS X 10.2.6, 10.3, 10.4
* CD-ROM drive
* Sound card
* Monitor displaying at least 800 x 600 pixels in 256 colors

TOP TIP
Now you're ready to design some outfits. Just follow the directions on the CD-ROM. If you get stuck, click on the "Help" button on the screen.

7

Get the look!

Chelsea wears...
BOHEMIAN BABE

Beth wears...
URBAN STYLE

Long beads

Chunky bangles

Peasant shirt

Pink hoodie

Diamont necklace

Motif joggers

Wide leather belt

Cowboy boots

Gypsy skirt

Funky sneakers

Cute purse

Fashion designers love to mix and match different items of clothing to create an overall look. Here's a quick lowdown on some of the latest trendsetting styles around.

TOP TIP
Start with a basic item, such as jeans, then add more items until you're happy with your look!

Scarlet wears...
PUNK GLAM

Kimberley wears...
CITY CHIC

T-shirt

Undershirt

Black leggings

Strappy sandals

Thin belt

Layered skirt

Floaty scarf

Cropped blazer jacket

Skinny-fit shorts

Shoulder bag

Camisole top

Ballet pumps

Try out the fashions within each season on the CD-ROM, then have fun mixing them up.

9

WARDROBE WONDERS

Fall days

Keep cozy in the fall months by layering up with different textures and earthy colors.

A gypsy skirt in warm browns or leafy greens is perfect for a hippie, country style.

GYPSY SKIRT

HOT LOOK!

Click on the "Add layer" button on the CD-ROM to team a funky T-shirt with a sleeveless top.

LOVELY LAYERS

Sleeveless top

Silky cardigan

Wide leather belt

Skinny jeans

Cowboy boots

10

Winter warmers

Winter clothes tend to be made from thicker fabric to keep out the cold. Go for funky knits and sturdy denims.

Roll-neck sweater

Cute poncho

PARKA JACKET

A parka jacket will keep you looking totally cool and feeling fabulously cozy.

Need something for BOTH daytime and evening winterwear? Go for a ballet top for versatility.

BALLET TOP

Boot-cut jeans

LOVE THE SHOES!

Ballet pumps

Spring fresh

Cool
cropped
jacket

Styles go back to
nature in the spring.
Catwalks are full
of pretty outfits in
pale purples and
daffodil yellows.

Skinny
belt

Stripes are
a classic look
for spring
and summer.

STRIPY TOP

Silk shift
dress

**CUTE
DRESS!**

Strappy
sandals

CHIC JACKET

A belted
jacket gives
a hint
of Parisian
chic during
springtime
showers.

Summer sizzlers

Summer fashion is all about keeping cool and having fun. Go for lighter fabrics and retro prints to hit the balmy months in style.

Superstar sunglasses

Polka-dot tube

FUNKY DRESS

A funky off-the-shoulder dress is just right for the beach and looks great teamed with jeans, too.

When the sun goes down, choose a short-sleeved jacket to keep you warm.

CUTE JACKET

Denim miniskirt

SO COOL!

Funky flip-flops

You can't beat a glam pair of sandals. They'll dress up your denim in no time at all!

Cowboy boots are a wardrobe classic! They look best with skinny jeans and miniskirts.

Shoes

Footwear can make or break an outfit, so choose your shoes carefully!

Flip-flops look great with everything— perfect for super sunny days.

Ballet pumps look cute with dresses. Add a polka-dot pattern if you want to jazz up a plain pair.

LOOKIN' GOOD!

For a cool 'n' casual look, try sneakers. Team them with black leggings and a miniskirt for a rock 'n' roll vibe.

A charm pendant will look pretty whatever the outfit. Heart and star charms are top of the fashion charts.

If you're looking for glam, you'll need some sparkle. Go for the ultimate bling accessory—a dazzling diamonté necklace!

BLING!

Chunky bangles in funky colors can look great with anything.

A bead necklace is THE accessory to be seen wearing. Black beads go with everything and look ultra-HOT.

Jewelry

Jewelry can help transform a plain outfit into a totally trendy look. Select the best accessories for your overall image.

Jingly bangles will give a cool edge to plain T-shirts and classic denim.

BEADS ROCK!

A thin patent belt can make a plain T-shirt look totally funky.

A glam clutch bag is perfect for partywear.

Bags & belts

Every girl needs a good bag and a funky belt to complete her outfit. But how do you go about choosing the right ones?

Want to give instant shape to a top or dress? Choose an ultra-trendy wide belt.

Canvas bags look best perfectly plain or prettily patterned. Experiment with different textures and patterns on the CD-ROM.

Across-the-shoulder bags look totally cool and feel fabulously comfy.

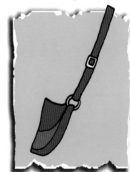

BAGS OF STYLE!

Sunglasses will protect your eyes from the sun AND make you look like a superstar. Cool!

Brrr! When the weather turns wintry, choose a woolly scarf to keep you cosy and looking super stylish to boot.

Bits & pieces

Supercharge your style by choosing accessories that best suit you and your personality.

For a funky '80s feel, leggings are just the thing! Wear them with short dresses, miniskirts, sandals, or pumps.

Gloves add instant glamor in the colder months. Choose cuddly knits or cute cord textures.

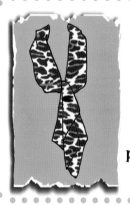

If you love dreamy designs, go vintage with a cool scarf. Pick pretty pastel colors or bold patterns that make a statement.

FUNKY PUMPS!

Super shades

Makeup is great for drawing attention to facial features. Not sure which eye shadow color to go for? Check out the shades below.

MODEL STATS

NAME: **Scarlet**
SKIN TONE: **Rosy**
EYE COLOR: **Green**
PERFECT SHADES:
Pastel pinks, blues, or greens

MODEL STATS

NAME: **Beth**
SKIN TONE: **Dark**
EYE COLOR: **Brown**
PERFECT SHADES:
Bright or creamy colors

MODEL STATS

NAME: **Kimberley**
SKIN TONE: **Olive**
EYE COLOR: **Brown**
PERFECT SHADES:
Smoky silvers or warm golds

MODEL STATS

NAME: **Chelsea**
SKIN TONE: **Peachy**
EYE COLOR: **Blue**
PERFECT SHADES:
Natural corals or aqua colors

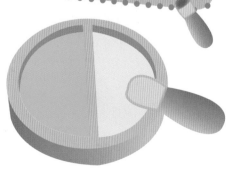

ULTIMATE GLAMOR!

Lovely lipsticks

Choosing lipstick can be tricky. If in doubt, stick to neutral shades and lip glosses that look good all the time.

DAY WEAR

Pinky neutrals look natural and moisturize lips, keeping them super soft.

PUCKER UP!

Ruby reds are ultra glam when worn with simple eye makeup.

PARTY TIME

Glossy nudes look great with shimmery eye makeup and sun-flecked blusher.

HANGIN' OUT

TOP TIP
Apply lip balm to soften your lips and create a smooth base for your lipstick.

Brilliant blusher

Blusher can add a lovely healthy glow to a pale complexion. Apply sparingly for a natural look.

Soft pink blush looks great on peachy and pink skins.

BIG-TIME BLUSHES!

Darker-skinned girls also look gorgeous in rosier shades of red.

Gold and bronze work well on girls with dark skin and olive tones.

Party polish

TOP TIP
Try not to paint your nails more than twice a week to keep them strong and healthy!

Painted nails will help to complete your look.
Check out these pointers for prettily polished nails!

BLINGIN' NAILS

RED HOT SHADES!

Glittery nails are perfect for parties.

Match lilac shades to bags and shoes.

Feeling bold? Check out cherry red.

Metallic blue is totally trendy.

Be pretty in pink, day or night!

HAIR FLAIR

Short & sweet

A fabulous hairstyle can totally transform your face.
Go for the chop if you're looking for a cool, edgy vibe.

PUNKY SPIKES
Choppy, spiky styles look ultra punky. Keep your
locks in place with hair gel or mousse.
PERFECT FOR: Round faces.

PIXIE CROP
Wispy layers will soften a super-short elfin
crop, making it look gorgeously girlie.
PERFECT FOR: Heart-shaped faces.

CUTE CURLS
Curly hair looks luscious in a choppy, short
hairdo, and won't take long to style in the morning.
PERFECT FOR: Long faces.

HOT STYLE!

LOVELY LAYERS
Pretty flicked out layers look modern and chic.
Side-swept bangs will keep the style looking soft.
PERFECT FOR: Oval faces.

Chin-length cutie

There are a lot of different ways to style chin-length hair. Choose a look that complements your face shape and hair type.

FUNKY BANGS

Heavy, blunt bangs give chin-length hair an ultra-modern dimension.
PERFECT FOR: Oval faces.

CHOPPY BOB

Loose bangs and a lot of choppy layers are a great way to wear chin-length hair.
PERFECT FOR: Any face shape.

WAVY BABE

Curly hair is big on volume. Cute little clips will help keep unruly strands in place.
PERFECT FOR: Any face shape.

SLEEK STYLE

For a super-trendy sleek style, dry your hair straight or invest in a pair of straighteners.
PERFECT FOR: Heart-shaped faces. **SO GLAM!**

Mid-length babe

You can get a different look every day with mid-length hair. Experiment with the styles that suit your face shape.

BOUNCY BUNCHES

Styling products add texture to curls. Tie your hair in bunches for a funky '70s look.
PERFECT FOR: Long faces.

TOO CUTE!

DO THE TWIST

Show off a dainty face by twisting your hair into a bun at the back of your head.
PERFECT FOR: Heart-shaped faces.

CRAZY CRIMP

Tie damp hair in a braid. Then, when it's dry, undo the braid to reveal a cool crimped style!
PERFECT FOR: Any face shape.

WISPY BANGS

Sweep wispy bangs to one side for a flattering, glamorous, film star look.
PERFECT FOR: Any face shape.

Long & luscious

Lucky long-haired girls have hundreds of styles to choose from. Which look suits your hair and face best?

PRETTY BRAIDS

Make sure your parting is straight, braid your hair, and secure it with funky hair accessories.

PERFECT FOR: **Any face shape.**

URBAN PONYTAIL

Gather your hair into an ultra-high ponytail. Use hairspray to smooth down fly-away strands.

PERFECT FOR: **Oval faces.**

SO SIMPLE!

PERFECTLY NATURAL

Give your hair a break from styling products and let it dry naturally after it's been washed.

PERFECT FOR: **Any face shape.**

BALLERINA BUN

It's easy to style curly hair. Pile it on top of your head, then pin your curls in place using grips.

PERFECT FOR: **Any face shape.**

BACKDROP BEAUTIES

Fashion shoot

Shoot location: THE BEACH

The beach is the ideal location to showcase your summer collection.

Shoot location: THE PARK

Show off spring fresh dresses, cute pumps, and floral bags in the park.

STRUT YOUR STUFF!

Clothes? Check! Shoes? Check! Jewelry? Check! Makeup and hair? Check! Check! Your models are finally ready to pose for the cameras! Which shoot location suits their look best?

Shoot location: THE CATWALK

Wow the crowds with your collection in the fall catwalk show.

Shoot location: THE CITY

This urban landscape screams attitude—great for cool, wintry shoots.

Print out your fabulous fashion pictures, then keep them safe in your very own fashion journal. Turn the page to find out more!

Cuts & clippings

When it's time to start work on a new collection, designers need plenty of inspiration. They collect together swatches of material, little sketches, and anything else that could be used for their new fashion designs.

Check out the cool outfits on the CD-ROM, then start designing your own range of clothes. Group your designs according to style and season.

TOP TIP
Use an old notebook or sketch pad for your designs.

HOT FASHION LOOKS

Spring: urban

Fall: bohemian

Winter: glam

Summer: chic

Texture is important to fashion design. Choose fabrics that look and feel great.

DESIGN DIVA!

Stuck for fashion ideas? Take photos of you and your pals in different outfits. Stick the photos in your design book and sketch some outfits based on your pics.

New collection